a
Christmas
Calamity

Freya Anduin
A Christmas Calamity

© 2024 Freya Anduin - all rights reserved.

www.freyaanduin.com

Cover background photo and layout: FP Anduin

ISBN: 97887-975723-0-6

Text, graphics, images, video, audio, and other content as part of, in or around this work is protected by copyright law. Freya Anduin reserves all rights to the content, including the right to utilise content, form, voice, etc. for the purpose of text and data mining or other forms of copying, sampling, reuse, etc. of the entire work or parts thereof, cf. Section 11 b of the Copyright Act and Article 4 of the DSM Directive.

first book in the series
Christmas at Merkantia

Other books by Freya Anduin

Into Their Stride
First book in the series
Lendorph & La Cour

www.lendorphandlacour.com

It was dark and quiet. Nothing stirred – not even a mouse. It wasn't because there was no one around. A large person was lying on the floor, but he wasn't breathing. He lay with his eyes open and looked very surprised. He had half a gingernut in his hand and crumbs in the beard.

When the night guard made his rounds, he didn't turn on the lights but just waved his torch about at the various sections of the department, so he didn't notice the person on the floor, partially hidden behind a sleigh piled high with presents. There was so much on display that it was impossible to spot anyone unless they were moving. There were gifts stacked in neat pyramids, a Christmas tree, a painted backdrop depicting Santa's workshop with a fireplace and everything as a set for elves of all sizes, apparently engaged in various whimsical tasks that would turn bits of painted wood into toys of the kind protruding from a giant sack next to the sleigh: dolls with corkscrew curls, giant nutcrackers painted like soldiers, teddy bears of all sizes... There was a big chair – almost a throne – with gilded carvings and purple velvet upholstery, and a table beside it with bowls of treats, and notably a large stack of wish lists, with several lines already filled in with the department store's gift proposals, so one only needed to tick a box. However, it was also possible to write something oneself. If you had your own pencil. There was a large basket where one could leave the wish list along with those of others and perhaps be lucky enough to win one of the pre-printed items on the list. There was one lucky winner every week.

Around the display were the usual shelves bulging with toys for children of all ages and in various price ranges from moderate to the equivalent of a country estate including church, park, and village.

The surroundings bore the marks of many visitors. The floor was adorned with candy wrappers, puddles of dirty water from melted snow, boot prints, lost mittens, a couple of pacifiers; an ear-flap cap had ended up under a shelf, and the goods on shelves below about a meter in hight seemed to have been handled by many hands. Dirty hands, mostly of the sticky variety, the result of sucking on candies too big to fit entirely in the mouth and therefore held in the hand, like the striped candy canes, which had been tentatively distributed to the children and then swiftly removed again, as some were left around when the curious child spotted something more interesting. Candies and canes had been replaced with gingernuts, which didn't have the same unfortunate effect; it took quite a bit of saliva in the crumbs before it got the gluelike stickiness of sugar and was, thus, not quite as big a danger to the toys on display.

A little before five, the cleaning ladies arrived so they could be ready on the dot. In contrast to the guard, they turned on all the lights and, therefore – though not immediately – noticed the person on the floor. And screamed. Very loudly and for a long time. This led to quite a gathering – primarily of other cleaning ladies, who joined the choir and contributed with both soprano and alto voices until a much stronger voice with knives in it joined in:

- *What* is going on here?

At which point everyone fell silent, and most of the spectators hurried back to where they came from, where scrubbers and the like were immediately put to use.

The owner of the authoritative voice strode into the Christmas display and discovered the cause of the screaming. The department store's Santa lay on the floor behind the sleigh and looked very red and very dead. The head housekeeper, Miss Kirsten Mikkelsen, very briefly got the same expression and complexion as Santa, after which hers changed to one more familiar to the staff, with pursed lips, narrowed eyes, red spots on the cheeks, and a swelling of the bosom, indicating the prospect of a voice of Wagnerian proportions. Miss Mikkelsen would have made a good Valkyrie. Right now, however, it was obvious it wasn't the department's cleaning lady who had dispatched Santa Claus to the eternal Christmas dinner as she had arrived only minutes before. She, along with the rest of them, was told to leave the area, after which Miss Mikkelsen returned to her office and her phone so she could call the police.

On the way, Miss Mikkelsen engaged in a lengthy conversation with herself about whether she should call the manager immediately or perhaps wait for the police, in the hope it might temper his apoplectic fit, which was inevitable when he discovered that there had been a murder in his Santa display. It couldn't be anything else, unless Santa Claus had choked on a biscuit, and since Mr Dam who inhabited the costume mostly consumed his meals in liquid form, that didn't seem likely. He insisted that at Christmas you had to be in high spirits – preferably those from a bottle.

She remembered that the manager had recently hired a house detective to keep an eye on light-fingered customers. Perhaps she should call him first. Her, she corrected herself. It was a lady. Perhaps a good idea, since most customers were women. Perhaps she should call the detective first in the hope of an explanation, avoidance of a crowd of policemen, cordons, and worse yet – a tremendous scandal. And an apoplectic fit. What was her name again? Something French... Miss Mikkelsen rifled through her phone book and found the number.

Private detective Adeline la Cour answered the phone from her bed and held the receiver a couple of inches away from her ear for the first few seconds until Miss Mikkelsen found the right volume fit for a phone call rather than reaching the back seats at the opera. Adeline listened attentively while a smile spread across her face almost to her ears. She understood the desire for discretion and promised to come immediately, and since Santa Claus couldn't get any deader, they could wait to call the police until they were certain it would be necessary. And the manager. Later.

The department store was not Adeline la Cour's only client. She had several assignments, some of which involved collaboration with the Detective

Department of the police, with whom she had inherited a good relationship. Her father had been a chief inspector and one of the best there had ever been. Her mother was still a sort of private detective, although she mostly dealt with very specific analytical tasks, where others, including the police's own laboratory, had given up, and only on a small scale. She had handed the business over to Adeline, who had been messing about in her mother's lab since she was nine. Mostly because it was impossible to keep her out.

Adeline had followed in her parents' footsteps in many ways – international education, skilled marksman, multilingual, intelligent, a good photographer, and – especially – a very good private detective. She had a knack for leaps of thought, the ability to take in a multitude of information at once and letting the mess crystalize into some kind of coherence, identifying individual pieces of a puzzle even when still a jumble in the box, pulling the thread until the knot became visible and could be untangled... Many metaphors had been used about her work, but the gist was that she was skilled – perhaps the best – and very, very discreet. The latter was not the least reason she never lacked assignments. Recently at the department store, there had been a bout of mysterious shrinkage of stock in departments where it normally wasn't possible, and where they suspected it might be individuals of a certain status who had their fingers on the wrong side of the counter. Something that needed to be stopped, but without scandal. And now there was a dead Santa. Moreover, the first of its kind. They had got the idea from New York, where Santa Claus had been popular for several years. Here, he was also already very popular and now, unfortunately, also very dead. Who on earth would murder a character who said ho ho ho all the time and handed sticky kids a cookie and a wish list?

Miss Mikkelsen had asked Miss la Cour to go straight to the toy department, where she was waiting, and she breathed a sigh of relief when she heard Adeline's footsteps approaching from the escalator.

She glanced at her watch. It was half-past five, and they opened at nine. With a bit of luck, the toy department would open too.

Adeline walked slowly and directly towards Santa's workshop, looking around to get an impression of the situation. Like the cleaning ladies before her, she found Santa lying behind the sleigh, but unlike the ladies, she refrained from screaming. Instead, she walked right up to him. She placed her bag on a stack of gift-wrapped boxes, knelt down, and sniffed at his mouth. Almonds. And port. She cautiously touched his very red cheek, half-hidden by the artificial beard. The red colour didn't rub off, confirming the suspicion of poisoning. Someone had done away with Santa.

It looked like he had been sitting on his throne, eating, and drinking, and had fallen forward, ending up lying between the throne and the sleigh. He must have consumed a considerable number of gingernuts and something else – there were more crumbs of a different colour. It was a large bowl, and there were only a few left. Next to it stood an empty bottle of port. Perhaps it was Santa's packed dinner? She cautiously examined his Santa suit. There was certainly enough room in the pockets for at least two pounds of biscuits and more than one bottle of port. Adeline walked up to Miss Mikkelsen, who had remained a few meters away.

- Probably cyanide poisoning, so it's a police matter. Shall I call someone I know? I can investigate the area but I'm not allowed to touch him.

Miss Mikkelsen nodded, and they went down to her office to make the call. Adeline called one of her father's oldest friends, who was still a detective – just. Chief inspector Anders Strøm answered the phone despite the hour, expecting work, and smiled when he heard Adeline's voice. She quickly explained the situation, and he promised to come immediately and bring the coroner. Adeline hung up and turned to Miss Mikkelsen.

- What's Santa's name?

- Karl Dam. He's normally a doorman. I'll try to find his file.

Adeline returned to the toy department to investigate further.

There was nothing to indicate anything other than the usual Christmas trade. It was only around Santa's chair that things were different. The gingernuts, the port, the crumbs on the floor... There was also an empty bowl with a napkin with lighter coloured crumbs in it. Adeline tasted them. There had been vanilla biscuits in the other bowl. She wondered if Dam had emptied that one too? There were no glasses, so Dam must have drunk from the bottle. It looked that way too. Someone had been sucking it. She brushed for fingerprints, of which there were quite a few. Even a full handprint.

She looked closer at the dead man and tried to imagine how he had fallen from the chair. He could have ended up on the floor without help by simply dropping to his knees and toppling sideways. There didn't need to have been anyone else nearby at the time. But why had he been sitting there, drinking, and eating biscuits? It must have been after closing time, otherwise he would have been reprimanded when some mother or nanny spotted the bottle and complained. And he must have brought some of the biscuits and certainly the port himself.

So, Santa had come in with his pockets full of biscuits and port, had settled in, eating, drinking, and had then fallen off the chair, dead from cyanide poisoning from something he most likely brought himself. She sniffed cautiously at the bottle. There was a hint of something other than port. Something more almond-like. The poison must have been in the port.

Why had Dam returned to the display? Why did he bring biscuits and port? Was it just for him, or did he have a rendezvous with someone? Did the person come? Did that person bring the bottle or one to be swapped with Dam's own? Why were there no glasses? Did they take turns drinking from the bottle? Had there even been others present?

Strøm and the coroner arrived and immediately went to Santa, where Adeline was waiting, and greeted her. The coroner confirmed the smell of bitter almonds and the red complexion, checked anything visible on the spot, and declared the man dead. Adeline had already photographed as much as she could. Strøm searched Santa's pockets and found a large empty crumpled pastry bag with vanilla biscuit crumbs in one pocket. The other contained a pair of white gloves, no longer all white, and a huge handkerchief. Maybe he'd had the bottle in it?

Something puzzled Adeline. The suit looked much too big – especially too long. Maybe it didn't matter when he just had to sit? Dam wasn't a big man, and certainly not fat. Under the Santa robe, he wore ordinary clothes; black trousers, a checkered shirt, brown shoes, and striped socks. He had a set of keys in one pocket – a front door key and a couple more, which could be for a cellar, a locker... There was no tag.

They took off his hat, and it was clear he wasn't a young man. He had dark brown hair with grey flecks at the temples, and he was balding at the crown. They removed the beard, which was hooked over the ears. He had sunken cheeks and stubble. He somehow looked wrong – apart from the colour. Adeline had been by just a couple of days before on one of her rounds and had also gone into the toy department to observe the customers there. She quickly found out it was a rather risky idea – at least if you valued your clothes. The children generally had no qualms wiping their fingers on the nearest coat and it wasn't always their mother's or the nanny's. She had also looked at Santa, who had seemed relatively tall and rosy-cheeked – not at all like this bloke. Was it Christmas magic that had made her see him as Santa, or was there another reason?

Miss Mikkelsen returned and explained that she couldn't find Dam's file, so that would have to wait. Dam was normally a doorman but had become Santa this Christmas after a competition in saying ho ho ho in the most cheerful manner in the department store's first attempt at having a Santa for the children. She glanced at the now unmasked Santa, gasped in confusion, and was obviously completely thrown.

- Who's that?

Three pairs of eyes looked questioningly at Miss Mikkelsen.

- Your Santa?

- No. That's not Karl Dam. I've never seen this man before.

But where was Karl Dam then? Had he also been murdered? Or was he the murderer? The coroner looked speculative.

- When did you close yesterday?

- At 10 o'clock.

- So, Karl Dam was here until 10 o'clock last night?

- Yes?

- What about the night watchman? – you have one, don't you?

- Yes. He does his rounds around midnight to make sure everything is closed and turned off, and there are no customers or staff left.

- So, either there was no one at that time, or this man has been lying dead without being noticed?

- He's hard to see until you get really close.

That was true. Adeline hadn't noticed him either until she stood next to him.

- Are you sure it was Dam who was here yesterday?

Miss Mikkelsen thought back to the moment she saw the man lying on the floor, where she just assumed it was Dam. It could have been someone else unless there was someone nearby who knew him. A bellboy would bring more gingernuts during the day, but not necessarily one who knew what Dam looked like – or who even looked at him.

- No. I'm not sure. I didn't realise it wasn't Dam when we found him, and I'm not here during opening hours – only from five to half-past nine, and the house is buzzing at Christmas, with everyone busy with their own chores. I don't think anyone would look twice at Santa if he was sitting here as he should.

- Is there a storage room nearby?

Adeline and Strøm looked at each other — they had thought the same thing. Maybe someone had wanted Santa out of the way, maybe just temporarily, while they got rid of this bloke, whoever he was.

- There are some storage rooms that way – otherwise, I don't know. I rarely come here; my office is on another floor. I think he has a room out there.

She pointed at a barely visible door.

- Do you have the keys?

Miss Mikkelsen rummaged in a pocket of her smock and pulled out a large bunch of keys. They went to the door, partially hidden behind both shelves and a curtain. It led to a small corridor, where there was a ladies' toilet, a broom closet, and a couple more rooms that Miss Mikkelsen had never looked into. Now she tried to open one of them, and succeeded.

In this room were boxes of Easter decorations and empty boxes labelled 'Christmas decorations' on the side. None of the boxes were large enough to fit anyone inside. They moved on to the next door, which was the broom closet, i.e., a room with all sorts of cleaning things, which looked just like expected, when the cleaning ladies had been to get the usual stuff about an hour ago. They opened the door to the toilet, which also looked as expected. Miss Mikkelsen was a little excited about what was behind the last door because she had never looked inside, so she had no idea what was there. She tried the door, which turned out not to be locked at all.

There was a chair, a wooden bench, a clothes rack with a few hangers, a small table with a mirror, and something that looked like theatre makeup, in front of a narrow, high-seated window. It looked like Santa's dressing room. On the floor lay a man either sleeping or unconscious, and Miss Mikkelsen instantly recognised him as Karl Dam, the man supposed to be Santa.

He was in shirtsleeves, trousers, and big black boots; his coat lay on the bench with his hat, a belt, and a large pillow, shoes neatly placed to the side. He seemed to have taken a blow to the head. Maybe with the nutcracker, which also lay on the bench. One of the very large wooden ones that looked like a soldier. Adeline fished a small glass bottle out of her pocket and held it under Dam's nose. He woke with a start and looked around confusedly, tried to sit up, grabbed his head, grimaced, groaned, and fell back again.

- Easy now. Just stay lying down. Miss Mikkelsen, you better call an ambulance. Meanwhile, we'll have a brief talk with Mr Dam here. You are Mr Dam, I assume?

- Two ambulances,

The coroner, who had followed them out of curiosity, interjected. Miss Mikkelsen nodded and left. Mr Dam tried to nod, but it was clearly not a good idea.

- Can you tell us what happened, Mr Dam?

The coroner officially concluded that this patient was alive and therefore not his problem, so he followed Miss Mikkelsen back to the dead man, whom he stripped of the Santa costume, which someone else would need sooner rather than later, and which could not provide any more clues anyway. He then sat on Santa's throne to wait for the ambulance to take the deceased to the Forensic Institute.

- I'll wait here.

Miss Mikkelsen went back to her office and called for ambulances.

Adeline had found a glass and fetched some water for Mr Dam, who drank greedily and after a while gathered himself enough to speak.

- You don't have anything stronger?

Adeline smiled at him.

- Do you drink a lot of port?
- It's cold outside.
- "But not in here.
- No. But after all the children... bbbrrrrrr...

He shook like a wet dog.

- You need it.

Adeline smiled again.

- What happened? How did you end up here? Like this.

- He hit me. ... With that.

Dam pointed to the nutcracker.

- So, you saw who?

- Don't know him. Bellboy, I think. Uniform.

Dam thought for a moment.

- He was... wrong.

- How so wrong?

- I don't know. Something. Can't say precisely. Maybe the way he walked. I don't know them. Only see them around.

- Where did it happen? In here?

- In the corridor.

Dam tried to look around without lifting or turning his head.

- Where's my costume?

- In the display. Were you in the department yourself yesterday?

What day is it?

- Tuesday.

- Yes. Until closing time. Then I went out here to take off the costume, as I usually do, and then... then that bellboy came and hit me.

- What time was that?

- Just past ten? I don't have a watch, but we close at ten, and I'm not allowed to leave until the last customer has left.

- Will you be able to recognise the boy?

- Maybe. I don't remember his face. Just that he looked wrong for a bellboy. Except for the uniform. And he had a nutcracker in his hand. That sort of drew attention.

Dam seemed exhausted from talking, so Strøm stopped asking, and he and Adeline stood in silence for a few minutes before they heard footsteps and opened the door to the corridor, so the ambulance people could bring in the stretcher. Dam was carried out, and Strøm and Adeline began examining the room.

- Maybe there are fingerprints in here?

Adeline retrieved her bag from the mountain of presents. There were plenty of fingerprints, but most likely Dam's own. There were also traces of blood – tiny dots from the door, confirming that Dam was hit in the corridor and then dragged inside. Further in, they found a blood smear where Dam had been lying. There were also two black streaks from the door across the floor, which could be tracks from Dam's rather heavy boot heels.

- He hasn't used the makeup, but he may have moved the chair to make room for Dam.

- I wonder if Dam was just supposed to be kept out of the way for a while, or if this was an attempted murder?

Adeline and Strøm collected what they could of evidence – fingerprints, dust from the floor, striped tissue paper of the kind wrapped around bottles from the bin, and agreed that there was probably nothing more to find – there were too many people using the corridor. The bottle and the nutcracker had been taken to Forensics. The cleaning ladies could start cleaning in the toy department, where there had also been too many people to find anything useful. The crime had to be solved in another way – and preferably very quickly. Now there were just over two hours until opening time.

It was quiet in the festively decorated staff canteen where Adeline and Strøm sat down and had a cup of coffee and a chat about what might have happened, starting with a summary.

- So, first Dam being Santa leaves the department to go home, gets hit on the head by someone dressed up as a bellboy, and is then dragged into his room. And at some point, later, someone who might or might not be the one who hit him, turns up and takes his costume, his biscuits, and his port, which he probably brought himself, judging by the paper in the bin. The new guy puts on the Santa costume, puts the biscuits and the port in the pockets, and sits down on

Santa's throne and enjoys some quiet time munching along, without knowing there is poison in – presumably – the port, which may have been in the dressing room since morning. And then he drinks enough poison to die from it, topples and is found by the cleaning ladies, but not by the guard because he was lying behind the sleigh.

- So, someone had a grudge against the original Santa, but is there one or two? One who wanted to get him out of the way, for – what? And one who wanted to kill him and could get to his bottle. But maybe the room isn't locked during the day. Surely no one comes that way, and the ladies hardly go there ... or do they?

- We must talk to his colleagues – the other doormen. And the bellboys. They should be arriving shortly, and they can also get breakfast here, so maybe we should just wait a bit...

That turned out to be true, as the canteen filled up, and it was fortunately easy to see who was who, by their uniforms.

- We don't have much time, so shall we take a group each?

Adeline nodded, got up, and went towards the bellboys. Strøm went to the doormen, who, like the bellboys, also helped with the morning refilling of shelves. They were happy to talk, as long as it didn't delay them, and they were happy to talk about Dam, who was a nice guy; a bit too fond of port and also a bit too fond of one of the girls in the sewing room. So fond she would soon need a larger dress size if he got their drift. Had it led to conflicts? Well, some, because he didn't seem to want to get married, and that didn't go down well anywhere. They had heard rumours that the girl wanted revenge, maybe something about getting him fired. It made sense to Strøm. Dam certainly could not do his job today, and that was hardly popular with management. No Santa just before Christmas? Did he have a replacement? Not as far as they knew. Did they know the girl's name? General shaking of heads. Something with M, probably.

It was hard to get anything useful from the bellboys. They had noticed nothing; they knew each other, and there had been no 'wrong' bellboy yesterday. There had been a uniform on a bench in their locker room this morning, which was unusual, as they all took good care of them. Otherwise, they would be docked pay, but none of them were missing one. They were made to measure in the sewing room right next door, where someone kept an eye on their keep, made sure they were washed and repaired, and if someone could no longer fit the uniform, which could also mean deductions in pay, and needed a larger one, a new one had to me made or maybe the old refitted if possible.

Normally you would advance to another function in the house before getting a paunch, explained one of them with a broad grin. Or find other employment elsewhere. It was best to be young, fast, and light on your feet. Also, in regard to tips.

- You look stupid in that uniform if you're too old.

- Will you show me your room?

It was not far from the canteen, and there was indeed a uniform on a bench. Adeline sniffed it. It smelled new and ... with a hint of perfume? Certainly not a hint of male. Considering how much they ran about; that was quite strange. It was warm in the department store and the uniforms were made of wool. Perhaps the wrong thing about the bellboy was that it was a bellgirl? Adeline examined the uniform. It looked like there was blood on the inside edge of a sleeve, as if it had run down the arm, and there was a spatter on the front of the jacket. Not easy to see on the dark burgundy fabric. The trouser legs looked like they had been under the heels. Too long for the one who had worn the uniform, meaning it couldn't have been the owner when they were made to measure. Adeline took it with her.

Strøm and Adeline met again in the canteen, where people were heading out to their workstations to get them ready for another very busy day. Adeline placed the uniform on the table. Strøm told about Dam's relationship with a seamstress, and Adeline about the uniform, and they agreed a seamstress would have access to the new uniforms, might even have sewn it herself, could put it on, put her hair up under the cap, and look enough like a bellboy in the hustle and bustle, where people saw the uniform and not the person, and follow Dam for revenge. Absence could get him fired – even if it was only once – and he was hit with a nutcracker, which wasn't exactly hard to find, as they stood in long rows on the shelves right in front of the door to the back passage.

   - But she probably didn't try poisoning him as well, even though the poison must have been meant for Dam. And who was the other Santa?

   Was there someone else who wanted to be Santa, who just took the chance to try it out in the dead of night? Or wanted to take over? Maybe saw Dam lying on the floor and who didn't expect to find him there at all but had assumed Dam had gone home? Maybe he thought he was dead?

The department store manager, who had now been informed, showed up with panic painted all over his face. Now there was only an hour till opening time.

- Can we open the department? Find another Santa?

Strøm nodded. There was nothing more to find at the crime scene and not in the dressing room, either. The suit bore no traces; the bottle and the rest of the biscuits were off to Forensics, so outwardly one could pretend nothing had happened.

- Yes. But there are more people we need to talk to. Is there an office we can use and someone who can help find people?

The director was so relieved, you could watch his jaw muscles relax.

- You can use my office. My secretary will assist you. Follow me.

They walked through the glittering department store, which was now buzzing with activity in the aisles with all kinds of goods. They had to weave between clothes racks and rolling carts. Adeline took the opportunity to ask who else had been considered for Santa, and was told by the manager that he actually didn't know, but his secretary did – or at least knew who to ask. He left them at the door to the office, where his secretary, Miss Jeppesen, welcomed them and instantly became friends with Strøm:

- Would you like some coffee?

The manager hastily disappeared before anyone noticed he was wearing pyjamas under his trousers and coat. Miss Jeppesen knew about the possible Santas because she had been on the committee that was to choose the right one. There had been Mr Dam, Mr Schou from the warehouse, Mr Hammerich from the bookkeeping department, Mr Meinertsen, who was a chauffeur, and another guard, Mr Mattsen. They had met Mr Mattsen; he was the one who had mentioned Dam's relationship with the seamstress.

- How many of them have keys to get around?

Miss Jeppesen wasn't sure.

- Schou and Meinertsen, perhaps. Hammerich would probably know where he could find some. But none of them have any business on that floor.

- What about the cleaning ladies? Which of them have keys?

- Old Mrs Anderson, of course. Maybe all of them. You'll have to ask Miss Mikkelsen about that.

- Do the staff interact with each other – like across departments?

- We have a club where they can meet. With lectures and theatre and the like. Language lessons. And a Christmas party and a summer outing, of course.

- So, Dam could have met the seamstress in the club?

Miss Jeppesen looked puzzled.

- What seamstress?

It obviously wasn't common knowledge that Dam had a relationship with a seamstress. Maybe it was best if Adeline visited them now, before rumours started. Strøm explained he had some phone calls to make, and that Miss la Cour would like to see the sewing room right now, if Miss Jeppesen would show the way?

The sewing room was large. Very large. Miss Jeppesen explained that there were over 200 employees, about half of them working from home, so finding someone who could be involved in the case wasn't straightforward. Adeline decided to use one of her father's methods – the nose. She remembered the scent of the bellboy uniform and walked around discreetly sniffing at the seamstresses, who were all busy and didn't look up. They were used to being watched, although it wasn't really necessary. There was an atmosphere of diligence and concentration, and it was obvious everyone knew what they were doing. Much was being made in the sewing room, including couture, which required over 50 dedicated seamstresses, but also alterations, refitting, monogramming bed linen, and the like.

In the couture department, there was also a lot of activity. Many of the city's socialites needed new dresses for Christmas and New Year, and not all of them were in good time. The couture show room opened at 11 am – society ladies didn't get up early, and the in-house createur, Monsieur Gênant, certainly didn't. Adeline quickly found out that perfume was not commonly used among seamstresses; their soap scents were different, and apparently, no one used real perfume. She ended up at the back of the couture department, where a tall, blonde girl stood by an evening gown in silver moiré draped on a mannequin pinning on a sleeve. If one looked closely – really closely – the shape of her slim figure revealed a hint of a bump on her stomach, barely visible under her smock, which was otherwise quite loose and with large pockets filled with various equipment, including measuring tapes, ribbons, and threads sticking out like snakes fleeing from a terrarium. She had a ribbon with a pin cushion around one wrist and another measuring tape around her neck.

Adeline walked over to take a look and stood so close to her that the girl automatically stepped aside. But it had been enough. Adeline recognised the scent. The question now was how to get the girl to come with her without causing too much of a stir, disrupting work. That wouldn't be popular. She gently took the girl by the elbow.

- Please come with me?

The girl looked terrified, but followed with no fuss. She seemed just as determined not to attract attention. Adeline stopped outside the door.

- Perhaps you should take off your smock, then no one will notice us.

The girl looked even more panicked, but took off her smock and wrapped the pin cushion in it, holding it tightly rolled under her arm as they continued towards the manager's office. When they reached the door, and it dawned on the girl where they were – easy to see on the large brass sign – she started to cry, and Adeline quickly ushered her inside and closed the door before anyone other than Miss Jeppesen could hear it. Strøm took out his handkerchief and handed it to her.

- What's your name, miss?
- Inger Münster.
- Sit down, please, Miss Münster, and blow your nose.

Miss Münster sat down, spotted the bellboy uniform at the other end of the large conference table, and fainted.

- Shall we take that as a confession?

Strøm chuckled. Adeline fished out the smelling salts from her pocket and revived Miss Münster.

- It seems you've seen the uniform before, Miss Münster. Maybe even worn it?

Miss Münster looked down at the table and nodded almost imperceptibly.

- Why, Miss Münster?

Silent and with tears streaming down her cheeks. Miss Münster clutched her stomach without registering it. Strøm and Adeline did. Mattsen had been right. She was pregnant, and maybe Dam was the father of the child.

- He was going to come in late and get fired?

Another almost imperceptible nod, this time followed by expert handkerchief wringing. Strøm was glad it was one of his new ones that could take the strain.

- Who else knew you were pregnant?
- I don't know.
- Have you talked to anyone about it?

Miss Münster shook her head.

- No one at all? Not even a friend?

Her gaze began to wander.

- Has he talked to anyone about it?
- I don't know.
- Do you know Mr Mattsen?
- Who?
- Do you know any of the other doormen?

A new headshake. Stronger this time.

- Do you know anyone outside of the sewing room? Besides Mr Dam, of course.

Miss Münster flinched when Strøm mentioned Dam's name.

- No.

Her gaze flitted again. So, it probably wasn't entirely true. The question was who she might have met, and according to Miss Jeppesen, it could be any other employee, so there was plenty to choose from. Both Strøm and Adeline were sure it was she who had knocked down Dam, and that Strøm had to take her in for further questioning. But was she a murderer? It wasn't Dam who had died. Adeline looked closely at Miss Münster. She was very pretty, almost classically beautiful, tall, slim and with slender, beautiful hands. Adeline thought of her mother and the photo studio she had grown up in, which was now hers. She imagined the darkroom. Cyanide. Used by photographers. Could Miss Münster have been photographed in some of the fantastic dresses made here?

- One moment.

Adeline went out to Miss Jeppesen and asked to see the latest catalogue. She rifled through it and sure enough; Miss Münster was photographed in some of the expensive evening gowns and, she had to admit, looked absolutely stunning.

- May I borrow this for a moment?

Adeline went back and placed the catalogue on the table, open on the evening gown spread featuring Miss Münster.

- Who is the photographer?

- I don't know his name.

Adeline looked at Miss Münster over the glasses she wasn't wearing and raised an eyebrow.

Miss Münster blushed and looked even more beautiful.

- Henrik Hertz.

Strøm and Adeline looked at each other. Aha. And it seemed Miss Münster knew Mr Hertz quite well. Hertzlich probably. They could almost see the pun hanging in the air and had to be careful not to smile. And he would have access to cyanide in connection with his work. Where she could also get hold of it if the photographs were from his studio.

- Where were the pictures taken?

- Here. In the show room. The dresses don't leave the house until they are sold.

- Do you often have pictures taken?

- When there are catalogues or advertisements.

- So quite often?

Miss Münster nodded. Strøm got up and went out to ask Miss Jeppesen if there was a room where Miss Münster could wait while they spoke to others? She nodded. The manager also had a private room – in fact, an entire flat – and Miss Münster could sit in his living room and wait, but it was necessary to have someone accompany her. The manager didn't want any of the staff alone in there, and there was also an entrance from the street, so it was possible to sneak out. Strøm nodded approvingly. Miss Jeppesen was quick, and she also managed to arrange for one of the office ladies to sit with Miss Münster, who was escorted into the manager's living room, which, just like his office, was totally devoid of Christmas decorations. Strøm went back to the manager's office and closed the door behind him.

- We might as well talk to that photographer Hertz. Could he be jealous of Dam?

- And the other wannabe Santas.

Miss Jeppesen made sure Schou, Hammerich, Meinertsen, and Mattsen were called for. The latter couldn't leave his post at the door, so he had to wait.

Hammerich turned out to be a small, skinny man with large horn-rimmed glasses who absolutely did not have Santa potential. He didn't know Miss Münster or Mr Dam and seemed credible enough, so he could leave. Meinertsen was out doing deliveries, so they eagerly awaited Mr Schou. Who didn't show up. Instead, a disgruntled warehouse manager appeared, explaining that Schou hadn't turned up for work this morning and thus, unfortunately, wasn't available for questioning. What did Mr Schou look like? Middle-aged, dark hair, greying at the temples, and thinning on top. Sinewy, narrow-faced, not very tall but strong. Why?

Adeline and Strøm nodded in unison. It sounded like Mr Schou had taken a turn as Santa all alone and had enjoyed himself with biscuits and port until he fell off the throne. Not from drinking, but from cyanide, even though a whole bottle of port would have made most people dizzy enough to fall over. It might have taken some time for the poison to take effect, but it would probably also take some time to eat at least a pound of gingernuts and vanilla biscuits, and there were only a couple left from the very large bag they had found in his pocket.

- I think we'll need you at Forensics. We have found someone who might be Schou.

Strøm picked up the phone and called the office, where they promised a car would come and pick up the warehouse manager and take him to the morgue to – hopefully – identify the deceased Santa, and that they would call back immediately when he had been there.

Miss Jeppesen once again proved to be quick-witted. Shortly after the warehouse manager had left with a constable, she knocked on the door and came in with a trolley with more coffee, rolls, sandwiches, pastries, and a selection of Christmas biscuits. An almost empty tray later, they called from Forensics and confirmed that the deceased was indeed Mr Schou and that his boss would notify the relatives.

- So, we still need to talk to the photographer.

- What about Miss Münster?

- Hmm. Perhaps she'd rather wait here than with the police?

They went out to Miss Jeppesen and asked her to call the couture department's manager. She handed the receiver to Strøm, who asked for photographer Hertz's address and was told that they could talk to Mr Hertz right here, as he was taking new photographs before the show room opened, and before Monsieur Gênant arrived and interfered with dresses that weren't his. Did he know what had happened to Miss Münster, whom no one could find and who was now missing as a model?

- We'll bring her.

Strøm called his own office again to ask for a couple of plainclothes detectives to take up positions outside the show room, in case Miss Münster should feel the urge to use the customer entrance as a staff exit. She couldn't get through the sewing room without being stopped. At the least to get the dress off her.

The couture show room's only decoration was a Christmas tree with gold ornaments, which had taken several days to decorate to Monsieur Gênant's satisfaction, or rather, grudging acceptance. Such frivolities didn't belong in his sacred halls and certainly weren't to be included in the pictures. Neither Strøm nor Adeline had any idea how cumbersome it was to photograph for a catalogue. How many people were involved in clothes, hair, makeup, draping, lighting... It felt like civilisations could rise and fall, maybe even entire universes, before anything happened, and you heard the first click of the shutter. But there were interesting moments – especially seeing the chemistry between Mr Hertz and Miss Münster. There were definitely herzen in the air, so they almost sparkled in competition with the Christmas tree ornaments. Perhaps that was what made the pictures so good?

They worked in absolute concentration until the last dress, after which Miss Münster was asked to change, and Mr Hertz looked around the room for the first time. He spotted Adeline and was completely stunned. Miss Münster was beautiful and... erm... well... so forth, but this one. That forehead. Those eyes. That hair. That chin. Aphrodite must have descended from Mount Olympus. If only he could find an apple, then he could be Prince Paris and correct that mistake back then... where was it... Troy? He looked around in confusion.

Strøm had been paying close attention and had to clench his jaw not to laugh. He agreed entirely with Mr Hertz that Adeline was exceedingly beautiful; a look she had after her father, and which she didn't care about at all. He gave her a glance and could see her cheeks vibrate with suppressed laughter. Adeline stood up to make sure Miss Münster didn't disappear, and the enchantment broke. Strøm took a chair and placed it in front of his own and gestured with a hand movement for Mr Hertz to sit down. He did. With a very disappointed expression and searching glances for Adeline, who was now out of sight.

- How well do you know Miss Münster?
- What? Why? Who are you?
- My apologies. Chief detective inspector Strøm. There has been an incident that I'm investigating together with the house detective.
- Who?

- Miss la Cour.

Strøm thought Adeline would probably have him trailing after her like a puppy – at least with puppy eyes, but as he knew her, she could handle him herself. If she wanted to. Strøm cleared his throat to bring Mr Hertz back from a little pink cloud, currently inhabited by himself and Miss la Cour. Strøm cleared his throat again. Mr Hertz really didn't want to leave his cloud.

- Miss Münster. You know her well?

Hertz still had a foggy look. Miss Münster? Who on earth was Miss Münster? Oh, her Münster. Do I know her? I know Miss la Cour. In a little while, at least...

- Mr Hertz!

Strøm's voice now had very sharp edges. He was thoroughly annoyed. He had sat still and watched dresses for over two hours, was thirsty after eating too much pastry, needed to pee, and wanted this case finished now. Hertz almost jumped in his seat.

- Sorry. Yes, I know Miss Münster.

- Privately as well?

Hertz looked like he was going to deny it, and, according to the changing facial expressions, ended up with the conclusion that it would be to no avail.

- Yes.

- Intimately?

- Yes.

- Do you know Mr Dam?

Hertz wanted to get up, but Strøm was quicker. He had almost 40 years experience in reading body language and could react to it before people themselves knew what they were up to. He had grabbed Hertz's arm before he had lifted his bottom even a centimetre.

- Were you here yesterday, Mr Hertz?

- No.

- Can anyone confirm that?

- I was at Dragsted all day photographing jewellery.

- And afterwards?

- In the studio. With my assistant.

Strøm cursed inwardly. If it wasn't Hertz who had poisoned Schou, who the hell had?

- Have you photographed Miss Münster in your own studio?

- Yes, of course.

Did he blush? Yeah... and a little redness appeared on the edges of the ears. I wonder what kind of pictures those were. So maybe Miss Münster had been looting the cyanide jar, after all.

- Wait a moment.

Strøm went out and found Adeline and Miss Münster and asked Adeline to pat down Miss Münster – person, clothes, and bag. Adeline also needed her reflexes and grabbed Miss Münster's wrist before she did anything but turn her head. She was taken back to the manager's office, where Adeline went through Miss Münster's pockets, and found a monogrammed handkerchief, a lipstick, and a small pale blue envelope containing a bit of white powder.

- What's this?
- Headache powder.
- Don't you need some now?

Adeline reached for a glass on the serving trolley and watched Miss Münster stiffen while she filled the glass with water.

- No?

Adeline walked towards her with the glass in one hand and the envelope with the powder in the other. Miss Münster backed away until she hit a table.

Adeline called the couture department and asked Strøm to come back with Hertz, who might be complicit, and it was probably time he took them both in for further questioning, preferably through the manager's private entrance at the back, so the Christmas spirit and especially spending wasn't unnecessarily challenged by uniformed police. But Adeline wasn't quite satisfied. Something was missing. Not quite right. She decided to take a walk in the basement.

Adeline found the Schou's locker room – and Schou's locker and his coat. It had been missing from the Santa set, which had made her believe he hadn't intended to stay or go home from there directly. Which didn't make sense before she'd had a rummage in his coat pockets. There she found a photograph of Miss Münster which certainly wasn't taken in the show room. The décor didn't exactly fit and neither did her clothing – or rather – the very artful lack of it. She was posing like a Greek statue and dressed accordingly in a very strategically placed piece of gauze. It was obviously taken in a studio as the backdrop was a Greek temple and landscape. How it had ended up in Mr Schou's pocket she had no idea. As she was putting the photo in her handbag one of Schou's colleagues came in and she took the opportunity to have a private chat about Schou. He had, apparently, had very high expectations lately and

Mr Christensen was certain he was up to something.

- He mentioned something about a plan, that would make him a lot of money. I think he mentioned some Christmas party or other.

Apart from that, he had no idea what Mr Schou was on about. They had no time to talk shifting goods and not much more in the canteen, where gobbling enough food to keep up was the important part rather than talking. And you couldn't really talk about someone when they were there, he added with a wink.

Adeline decided to go back to the manager's office and have another look in Miss Münster's handbag which had been left behind.

It took some time and emptying the handbag completely before a thorough inch by inch feel of the lining revealed something hidden in it. There was a letter. From Mr Schou.

A couple of days later, Strøm was having dinner with his best friends and their daughter Adeline and, at coffee and petit fours, he entertained the company with how things had progressed.

Mr Dam had recovered and explained that Miss Münster had claimed he was the father of her child, but he had counted on his fingers and it didn't add up, so he neither wanted to marry her nor have anything further to do with Miss Münster. She had kept trying to contact him – that's why his colleagues knew something was going on. It could be true that she followed him in the bellboy's uniform – she was tall enough to pass for a young man, and she was athletic – she was a champion swimmer – so she had the strength to hit him on the head with the very heavy nutcracker and afterwards drag him into the dressing room. Dam hadn't recognised her, because, as he had said when they found him, his attention was completely focused on the nutcracker. He didn't know Schou – not even when shown a picture.

Miss Münster had stubbornly insisted that Dam was the father, but eventually had to admit she wasn't sure – it could just as well be Mr Hertz... or someone else. Strøm explained how he had been to Hertz's studio and found a whole series of photographs of Miss Münster, who had an unusually beautiful figure and looked fantastic in various classic poses wearing a minimum of delicately draped gauze, alternatively standing next to a palm frond with a strategically placed leaf. All very tasteful. Very classical. He pulled out a couple of photographs from his pocket and passed them around.

- She should model for a sculptor.

Strøm regretted it might take a while, as she would face trial for murdering Schou. During a visit to Hertz's studio and after a series of classical photographs, she had gone with him into the darkroom, had spotted a blue glass jar on a shelf, thought it was pretty, and had taken it down to look at it, after which Hertz had torn it out of her hands with an explanation that she mustn't touch it, because the content was poisonous. She remembered that, and only the day before the murder, she had helped herself to the powder in the jar without knowing what it was.

Miss Münster had put a small amount in an envelope, which she had taken to work, expecting it to be rat poison. She knew where Dam's dressing room was, knew about his habit of keeping bottles of port there, and poured a little powder into a bottle. She became unsure if it was enough to make him sick and decided to ensure an effect by also giving him a wallop with one of the nutcrackers conveniently at hand, and since she had seen the bellboy uniform in the sewing room shortly before, it gave her the idea to disguise herself just to be on the safe side. It wasn't her intention for Dam to die. Just to be fired.

- Do you believe that?

Strøm looked at Adeline, who laughed.

- Nah, not entirely. Schou didn't have his coat with him at the toy department, so I had to go down to the locker room to find it, and guess what I found in one of the pockets? One of Hertz's photographs of Miss Münster – one of those with the draped gauze. Which, by the way, turned out to be from the sewing room. I had a chat with one of Schou's colleagues, who informed me that Schou had 'a plan' that would pay for his Christmas celebrations. He didn't know what it was about, but Schou had seemed very excited. So, I took a closer look at Miss Münster's handbag, which turned out to have a letter hidden in the lining. From Mr Schou. A very friendly letter, offering her aforementioned picture for only 300 kr. and a little affection.

Strøm looked approvingly at Adeline and added.

- We presented the letter and picture to Miss Münster and she reluctantly admitted to arranging a meeting with Mr Schou at the Santa set up – it's an easy place to find – to complete the little deal. She knew perfectly well what was in the blue jar, and it was definitely her intention for Schou to die. She expected – probably quite rightly – that the 300 kr. would be just for starters.

- But Dam was only supposed to be fired.

- And temporarily out of the way while it looked like the poison was intended for him. Miss Münster also had a plan.

- So, she knocked out Dam, dragged him into the dressing room, took off the bellboy uniform, poured the poison into the port, and took the bottle, the biscuits, and the costume into the Santa display, just before Schou showed up. Miss Münster then charmed Schou, who clearly had high expectations of what he would receive from Miss Münster besides the 300 kr. He began to make advances, and Miss Münster led him on: got him to put on the costume, beard, and everything, and sit on the throne, so she could 'sit with Santa', and he had been mesmerised and probably couldn't believe his luck, as he had also wanted to be Santa himself. And then she sat on his lap and kissed him and gave him port and biscuits and promised all sorts of things until he became dizzy, and she promised even more tomorrow while she watched him get increasingly short of breath and eventually stopped breathing altogether. Then she left him lying on the floor an went to take the bellboy uniform back to their locker room before she went home. That's what she said. Eventually.

It was correct that Hertz kept cyanide in an unlabelled blue jar he still used for his artistic high quality cyanotype images, but since he was the only one who entered the darkroom, he didn't think it mattered. He didn't know Miss Münster had helped herself to a spoonful and that was possibly correct, but she had actually asked what was in the jar. He got a fine for not labelling the jar as poison, but they couldn't pin anything else on him. They couldn't prove he was privy to Miss Münster's plans, and since it would have been extremely risky for her tell him, they had taken his claim to ignorance at face value.

Adeline had received an extra Christmas bonus. The manager was very pleased with the quick resolution but considerably less pleased that their best couture model was now incarcerated for murder. At least there had been no damage to the Christmas decorations or any disruptions in the booming trade. Life in the toy department was as busy, loud, and sticky as ever. Dam was back as

Santa two days later, but had for some reason lost his taste for port.

Laughter spread around the table. Strøm raised his glass.

- To Santa.

Next book in the series

Christmas at Merkantia

will be

Murder a la Mode

Maybe you will also enjou

Into Their Stride

First book in the series

Lendorph & La Cour

Have a taste:

Editor of Aftenbladet, Bærentzen, sat at his desk, tapping his fingers on the table, quite unsure if he was about to make a mistake. According to the appointment, there were only a couple of minutes left until a Miss Anna Lendorph would walk through the door as an applicant for a journalist position. A woman in a newsroom? Rasmussen would be against it, no doubt about it, but it wasn't his decision; in fact, he wasn't even told. However, Miss Lendorph had the language skills Bærentzen needed, and no men had applied on such impressive qualifications.

    The sound of the front door made him look up, and there she was. Young, red-haired, elegant in a smart suit with matching hat, sharp grey-green eyes... hmm... perhaps not the worst idea after all. He rose to welcome her and asked her to sit down.

- You're an academic, I see. Not strictly necessary, but your language skills are precisely what I'm looking for. You mentioned you've been to boarding schools in both Switzerland and England?

- Yes, although only a couple of years at each place. Enough to speak French, Italian, and English fluently. German, of course, I already knew – as do most, I suppose.

- Excellent. What I need is someone capable of reading foreign newspapers and telegrams and find the right pieces for Aftenbladet's readers – and reproduce them in our style. Not translate, but write based on the information from, say, Figaro.

- I'm sure I can do that to your satisfaction.

Editor Bærentzen still looked unsure. Anna, on the other hand, was anything but. Bærentsen needed a little more to be certain.

- You know that it's primarily crime stories that catch the readers' attention – which can be a bit... gruesome?

- Of course. But I take a personal interest in crime stories – I must admit, I read both Émile Gaboriau – You know Monsieur Lecoq, I presume?

– and Conan Doyle, of course. And not just because he is my great-uncle.

- You read Sherlock Holmes? And are related to Conan Doyle?

Bærentzen had a hard time hiding his enthusiasm.

- Yes. My grandmother is English and related to his mother – and perhaps soon even more – his brother is courting Clara Swendsen, who is also family. I have met him a couple of times in London and visited him at Windlesham.

That dispelled the last shred of doubt. For a former freelance crime reporter, it was the perfect bait. Conan Doyle's niece or something. Bærentzen was almost star-struck.

- Well then, I expect you to be familiar with criminology and all its challenges – and that it will be routine to describe foreign events accurately.

- Elementary.

Anna couldn't resist, even though it was silly. But the effect was the intended. The decision had been made; it was evident in the changed tone and expectant look, even though they were being suppressed. Anna noted the change with satisfaction. Her homework had paid off.

- What else do you do besides reading?

- Fencing. Pistol shooting – on a range, of course. I attend a lot of theatre and lectures, mostly scientific.

Bærentzen was impressed against his will.

- Well then. Are you engaged, Miss Lendorph?

- No. I've been busy with my education and have travelled a lot. I'm in no hurry.

That was true enough. No need to elaborate that marriage held absolutely no interest. End up as a man's personal property? No way.

- Excellent.

A sweeping gesture indicated it was time to meet the rest of the editorial staff, which as this particular time turned out to be one very disgruntled male journalist. Bærentzen and Anna went out into the newsroom – a smallish room with wood panelling, a large world map, shelves with various books, including dictionaries, stacks of used and unused notepads, and something that looked like a trophy. The general lighting was unimpressive, but there were proper lamps on the desks in the classic design – brass and green glass.

Bærentzen pointed to an empty desk with a leather chair imprinted with a bottom as padded as the chair, an older model telephone, and – evidently no expense spared – the very latest in typewriters: the best and newest Remington with key-set tabulator. There was also a tray stand and a mysterious sharp metal object that looked like a spike on a wooden block.

- This will be your desk.

Anna glanced at the other desks to see if there was anything to illuminate the function of the spike. They all had a similar contraption with paper impaled on it. To do spike or wastepaper basket? That would have to wait.

Bærentsen regained attention with an introduction to the older colleague. A middle-aged, thin-haired, bespectacled gentleman in a brown suit, a hideous tie in rusty red colours, and a musty facial expression, partially hidden behind a beard.

- Carl, this is Miss Lendorph. She'll do our foreign affairs. Miss Lendorph – journalist Carl Rasmussen. He also writes our serials under the pseudonym Jens Hammer.

Mr Rasmussen was clearly unenthusiastic, although he attempted a grimace vaguely resembling a smile. Anna smiled back and extended her hand.

- How do you do, Mr Rasmussen?

He managed a surprisingly limp handshake. Both Rasmussen and Anna were relieved that their areas of work were entirely different and did not entail cooperation of any kind.

⁂

Almost simultaneously and not far away, another conversation similar to the first was initiated. Police sergeant Christian la Cour had had a talk with his superior, police inspector Hakon Jørgensen, who had suggested he applied for the vacant position in the Detective Office of the Copenhagen Police. Not that Jørgensen wanted rid of him, but he had abilities. At 29, he was mature enough, and for Christian, it was both a promotion and a challenge, although his time with Jørgensen had been quite extraordinary. So, now he sat in front of Assistant Commissioner of Police, Henrik Madsen, head of the Detective Office. A tall, middle-aged man with cropped, grey hair, a military style moustache, and a gaze that clearly indicated he could not be fooled.

- So, you want to be a detective?

- Yes. I believe I have the abilities. At least, that's what my inspector thinks. He was the one who brought this opportunity to my attention.

- I see... Your background is somewhat unusual?

- I have completed my military service as a guardsman, and I've been at Nørrebro police station for three years.

- Of course. But ballet?

- Yes, I've been a principal dancer. Had to leave because of an injury that would have left me disabled had I continued.

The last remark elicited a smile from the chief.

- The ballerina was too heavy? You know that a certain physical standard is expected? But I suppose you already know from Nørrebro.

- I can throw a left hook too, should I need it.

Henrik Madsen's smile turned into a chuckle:

- I didn't know one got into scuffles in the corps de ballet?

Christian grinned back:

- You'd be amazed, sir. But it was mostly outside. Being a boy attending ballet classes in my neighbourhood was tougher than being a constable.

- Yes, I can imagine. And did you develop a left-handed combat technique there?

- Let's just say, I got good at avoiding a beating and gained a certain reputation for using... lesser-known techniques...

Madsen took a closer look at his applicant. Young, tall, dark-haired, brown eyes, almost girlishly handsome and unusually well-built. And according to Jørgensen, someone the diverse clientele who occasionally took a short, involuntary break at Nørrebro Police Station had a lot of respect for. Perhaps because he could carry most of them in one arm while they struggled to touch the ground.

- Yes, you certainly seem to be in good physical shape. Anything else I should know about you?

- I'm familiar with police work in Paris and their new methods. Besides French – because of ballet – I also speak German and English.

- Indeed. Why the English?

- I learned English by reading Sherlock Holmes in the original language, and took classes because I considered going to America with Ingeborg, my former fiancée. We studied together. Then she left and I didn't.

- And now you want to be the Sherlock Holmes of Copenhagen?

Madsen couldn't resist a hint of sarcasm, even though Jørgensen had assured him that sergeant la Cour was well qualified.

- More like Monsieur Lecoq, sir. I'm used to working within the police force.

And good at speaking up for himself, Madsen had to acknowledge. He resolved to follow Jørgensen's advice.

- Excellent. We can certainly keep up as well. Our Central Bureau of Identification is greatly admired throughout Europe, and right now, we have a success rate of 100 per cent. I look forward to your contribution to raising the standard even further. Talk to Senior Inspector Schou; he will give you your new badge and a copy of the Instructions and Gross' handbook on criminal investigation, which I expect you to read as soon as possible, and which may show you that Mr Holmes isn't as unique as one might think. I assume you are well-versed in police regulations? Schou will also meet you when you start on duty and, among other things, take you to the laboratory, the museum, the Central Bureau, and to the Institute of Forensic Medicine, with whom you will collaborate.

- Of course.

- You can hand in your uniform at your station – we dress in plain clothes. A desk will be ready for you on Monday. You are now officially among the best in the police force. We expect you to perform accordingly.

Madsen watched Christian as he left the office. Poised – in a police uniform. Something didn't quite add up, but it would only be for a few more days. He would look natural in civilian attire, and – one could hope – would be fully capable of a top performance on manners and good conduct, which were the top brass' new favourite words, besides being tough, which was just as necessary even though things were changing.

Madsen remembered Jørgensen's explanation: 'He can give them a wallop and lift the rascal into the wagon with one arm, while being the picture of kindness, so they're almost thanking him for the arrest. Never seen anything like it.' That sounded promising. The challenge now was to place him. He didn't resemble any of the others and might come off as provocative to some. A bit too elegant. A bit too... different. Especially intelligent, if one were to believe Jørgensen.

For now, he decided to let him have a desk to himself with no one opposite until he could see how it went. The gossip would start immediately, no doubt about it – no one can gossip like policemen – and then he would see how la Cour handled it. And soon, there would come yet another new officer, who, apart from the intelligence, was almost his opposite. A country boy who would be just as different, only differently different. Both would need a partner. Detectives worked best in twos. They would encounter things on the job that would be easier to bear if they were two to talk. Two who knew what they had seen. But first, Schou had to take care of la Cour and get him up to speed. They would get along well, he was sure. Same with Bugge at the Central Bureau. It would all work out fine.

...

Available at webshops around the world.

Milton Keynes UK
Ingram Content Group UK Ltd.
UKHW041822131124
451149UK00001B/20